This

# never land Journal

belongs to

_____

Date _____

ISBN 978-0-553-49685-7
randomhousekids.com
Printed in the United States of America
10 9 8 7 6 5 4 3 2 1

# DISNEY
# The Never Girls

# my never land Journal

Written by Kristen Depken
Based on the series by Kiki Thorpe
Illustrated by Jana Christy

A Stepping Stone Book™
Random House 🏠 New York

# All About Me

Each of the Never Girls is unique—
and so are you!
Write all about yourself in this journal.

My name is _____.

I am ____ years old.

My birthday is

_____.

My hair color is

_____.

My eye color is

_____.

I am ____ feet ____ inches tall.

Draw or paste a picture
of yourself here.

# My Family

Mia and Gabby are sisters.
What is your family like?

My parents' names are _____

_____

_____.

I have _____ brothers.

Their names are _____

_____

_____

_____.

I have _____ sisters.

Their names are _____

_____

_____

_____.

The thing I love most about my family is _____
_____
_____
_____
_____
_____
_____
_____
_____
_____
_____.

Draw or paste a picture
of your family here.

# The Thinkers

What are Gabby and Mia thinking?

Write your ideas here.

# Fairy Mail

Mia writes a note for Prilla to deliver to her parents. Pretend you are visiting Never Land. What would you write home about? Finish the letter any way you like.

Dear _____,

    Never Land is so _____

_____.

I've met lots of nice fairies, including _____

_____ and _____.

The strangest thing I've seen is _____

_____

_____

_____.

I really love the _____

_____

_____

_____.

Dear Mami and Papi,
How are you? We are fine. We are
Visiting in Never Land. It's nice here.
Please tell the other moms don't worry.
Love, Mia, Gabby, Lainey, Kate

I've had the most fun _____

_____

_____

_____

_____.

The thing I miss most from home is _____

_____

_____

_____

_____.

Love,

_____

# My Home

Never Land fairies live in a big maple tree.

What is your home like?

I live _____

_____

_____.

The best way to describe my home is _____

_____

_____

_____

_____

_____

_____

_____

_____

_____

_____.

Draw or paste a picture
of your home here.

# My Room

In Pixie Hollow, the Never Girls have a room in a willow tree!

Write about your room here.

The word that best describes my room is

_____.

My room is decorated with _____

_____

_____

_____.

The colors in my room are _____

_____

_____.

If I could change one thing about

my room, it would be _____

_____

_____.

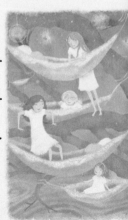

# Draw or paste a picture of your room here.

# My Favorites

Gabby's favorite ice cream is rainbow sherbet.

Mia's favorite color is pink.

My favorite color is _____

_____

_____.

My favorite food is _____

_____

_____

_____.

My favorite book is _____

_____

_____

_____.

My favorite actor is _____

_____

_____.

Write about your favorite things here.

My favorite season is _____

_____

_____ .

My favorite sport is _____

_____

_____ .

My favorite sports team is _____

_____

_____

_____ .

Draw a picture of your
favorite Spot in your home.

My favorite song is _____

_____

_____.

My favorite word is _____

_____

_____.

My favorite flower is _____

_____

_____.

My favorite holiday is _____

_____

_____.

# Crazy About Animals

If you could have any animal as a pet, what would it be? _____

_____

What would you name your pet? _____

_____

What tricks would you teach your pet? _____

_____

_____

_____

If you could talk to animals, what would you say? _____

_____

_____

_____

_____

What animal would your parents not want in

the house? _____

_____

_____

_____

_____

Why not? _____

_____

_____

_____

_____

_____

_____

_____

# My Hobbies

Whenever she gets the chance, Tinker Bell
likes to tinker in her workshop.

Write down three things you like to do in
your spare time.

1. _____

_____

2. _____

_____

3. _____

_____

# Write down three things you would like to learn how to do.

1. _____

_____

_____

2. _____

_____

_____

3. _____

_____

_____

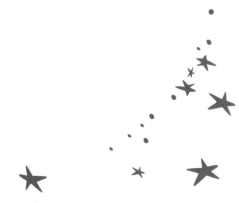

# You're #1!

Every fairy in Pixie Hollow has a talent.
It's the thing she does best and loves to do more
than anything else. What is *your* special talent?

## Draw a picture of it here.

The Never Girls love to explore new parts of Never Land. Do you like to travel?

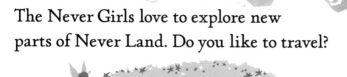

Write about a time you
traveled to a new place.

_____

_____

_____

_____

_____

_____

_____

_____

_____

Make a list of the places
you want to travel to someday.

★ _____
★ _____
★ _____
★ _____
★ _____
★ _____
★ _____

# Deep Thoughts

What do you suppose Kate is thinking?

Write your ideas here.

Rosetta feels sad when she sees a wilted garden.

I feel sad when _____

_____

_____

_____

_____

_____

_____

_____

_____.

Gabby is happiest when she's with the fairies.

I feel happy when _____

_____

_____

_____

_____

_____

_____

_____

_____ .

Gabby never goes anywhere without her beloved fairy wings.

What is your most prized possession?_____

_____

_____

Write about why it is special to you.

_____

_____

_____

_____

_____

_____

_____

_____

_____

_____

_____

Draw a picture of your most
prized possession here.

Write about
a person you
really admire.

_____

_____

_____

_____

_____

_____

Draw a picture
of them here.

Write down three things
you do well.

1. _____
_____
_____

2. _____
_____
_____

3. _____
_____
_____

When the Never Girls are home, they can't wait until their next trip to Never Land.

Write about something you're really looking forward to.

_____

_____

_____

_____

_____

_____

_____

_____

Fairies love to dance!

My favorite song to dance to is _____

_____

_____

_____ .

I like to dance with _____

_____

_____

_____

_____

_____

_____

_____

_____

_____

_____ .

## Ingredients

_____

_____

_____

_____

_____

_____

_____

_____

_____

_____

_____

# Directions

_____

_____

_____

_____

_____

_____

_____

_____

_____

_____

_____

_____

One thing I can't live without is _____

_____

_____

_____

_____.

_____

_____

_____

_____.

_____

_____

_____

_____.

Sometimes a day just doesn't go right.

What do you do to feel better when you've had

a bad day? _____

_____

_____

_____

_____

_____

_____

My biggest fear is _____

_____

_____

_____

_____

_____

_____

_____

_____

_____

_____

_____

_____ .

Lainey never expected to meet new children
in Never Land!

Write about a time when
you met someone new.

_____

_____

_____

_____

_____

_____

_____

_____

# Delightful Daydream

What do you suppose Gabby is thinking?

Write your idea here.

My
Friends

Friends come in all shapes and sizes—some are even fairy-sized!

My best friends are _____

_____

_____

_____

_____.

I like them because _____

_____

_____

_____

_____

_____

_____

_____

_____

_____.

Draw or paste a picture of you
and your friends here.

What do you and your friends have in

common? _____

_____

_____

_____

_____

How are you and your friends different from

one another? _____

_____

_____

_____

_____

_____

_____

_____

I have the most fun with my friends when we

_____

_____

_____

_____

_____

_____

_____

_____

_____ .

# Quiz: Which Never Girl Am I?

1. I would describe myself as:
   A) a leader
   B) a girly girl
   C) a good friend
   D) a fairy

2. My favorite thing to do is:
   A) climb trees
   B) get dressed up
   C) cuddle with animals
   D) play make-believe

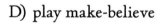

3. My friends would say I'm:

    A) adventurous

    B) outgoing

    C) shy

    D) silly

4. My favorite outfit is:

    A) jeans and a T-shirt

    B) a pretty dress

    C) pigtails and glasses

    D) a tutu and fairy wings

5. If I went to Pixie Hollow, I would:

    A) explore all of Never Land

    B) go to a fairy party

    C) talk to animals

    D) play hide-and-seek

If you answered with:

**Mostly As:** You're Kate! You love adventure, excitement, and exploring the outdoors.

**Mostly Bs:** You're Mia! You love dressing up, throwing parties, and admiring the beauty around you.

**Mostly Cs:** You're Lainey! You love animals, nature, and spending time with your friends.

**Mostly Ds:** You're Gabby! You love magic, make-believe, and making dreams come true.

# What do you and your friends do when you're together?

Write about it here.

_____

_____

_____

_____

_____

_____

_____

_____

Write about a time you helped a friend.

_____

_____

_____

_____

_____

_____

_____

_____

_____

_____

_____

_____

_____

_____

Write about a time a friend helped you.

# Story Time

As they wait out the storm, Gabby tells
Iridessa a story. Write your own story below.

Once upon a time, there was a _____

named _____

who lived in a place called _____

_____ .

She/he was very _____

and loved to do all sorts of things, such as_____

_____

_____

and _____

_____

_____

_____ .

One day she/he met a _____

_____ .

Together, they _____

_____

_____

_____

_____

_____

_____

_____

_____

_____

_____

_____. And they lived happily ever after.

Write about a time you got mad at your friends.

_____

_____

_____

_____

_____

_____

_____

_____

_____

_____

Write about the best time you ever had with your best friend.

_____

_____

_____

_____

_____

_____

_____

_____

_____

_____

_____

_____

_____

_____

# What games do you play with your friends?

Write about them here.

_____

_____

_____

_____

_____

_____

_____

_____

_____

_____

_____

_____

_____

# Fairies

The best part about visiting Never Land is meeting the fairies.

What would you do if you met a real fairy?

_____

_____

_____

_____

_____

_____

_____

_____

_____

_____

_____

Every fairy has a special talent.

If you were a fairy, what would your talent be?

_____

_____

_____

How would you use your talent? _____

_____

_____

_____

_____

_____

_____

_____

_____

_____

_____

My favorite fairy in Pixie Hollow is _____

_____

_____.

I like her because _____

_____

_____

_____

_____

_____

_____

_____

_____

_____.

Gabby drew this picture of Tinker Bell.

## Draw a picture of *your* favorite fairy here.

Sometimes the magical passageway to Never Land is between the slats of a fence in Mia and Gabby's backyard. Sometimes it's in Gabby's bedroom closet.

If there were a portal to Pixie Hollow in your

home, what would it be? _____

_____

Where would it be? _____

_____

_____

If you could spend the day in Pixie Hollow,
what would you do?

_____

_____

_____

_____

_____

_____

_____

Throw a pixie party! If you threw a party for fairies, what would it be like?

Food: _____

_____

_____

_____

_____

Decorations: _____

_____

_____

_____

_____

_____

Games: _____

_____

_____

_____

_____

Music: _____

_____

_____

_____

_____

_____

_____

_____

_____

_____

# You're a Fairy!

What kind of fairy would you like to be?
Use your imagination and fill in the blanks.

Your fairy name: _____

_____

Your fairy talent: _____

_____

_____

Describe your fairy outfit: _____

_____

_____

How would you decorate your room in the

Home Tree? _____

_____

_____

_____

_____

What fairy food would you most like to eat?

_____

_____

_____

Which fairies would you most want to be

friends with? _____

_____

_____

Draw a picture of yourself as a fairy!

# welcome to Never Land

Imagine you're in Never Land.

Draw yourself in the scene below.

Fairy dust helps the fairies and the Never Girls fly!

If you had a teacup full of fairy dust, what would you do? _____

_____

_____

_____

_____

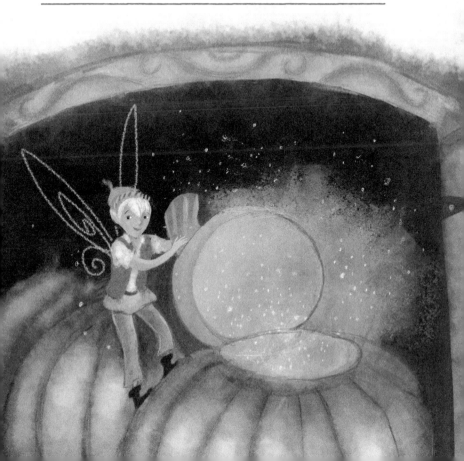

The animal-talent fairies are teaching Lainey how to talk to animals.

If you could talk to animals, what would you say?

_____

_____

_____

_____

_____

_____

_____

Every fairy has a unique pair of wings.
If you had wings, what would they look like?

Draw them
here.

Never Land

Torth Mountain

Pixie Hollow

Skull Rock

Mermaid Lagoon

Pirate Cove

The part of Never Land I'd most like to visit is

_____

_____

_____

_____

_____

_____

_____.

Silvermist is a water-talent fairy.

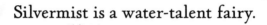

Draw your favorite spot with water.

Don't forget to put yourself in the picture!

Vidia is a fast-flying fairy.

I go fastest when I _____

_____

_____

_____

_____

_____

_____

_____

_____

_____

_____

_____

_____ .

Bess is an art-talent fairy.

My best creation is _____

_____

_____

_____

_____

_____

_____

_____

_____

_____

_____

_____

_____

_____ .

Prilla has a unique talent—she can travel to the mainland on a blink.

I'm unique because _____

_____

_____

_____

_____

_____

_____

_____

_____

_____

_____

_____ .

Tinker Bell is good at fixing things.

One thing I wish I could fix is _____

_____

_____

_____

_____

_____

_____

_____

_____

_____

_____

_____

_____.

Dulcie is a baking-talent fairy.

My favorite food to make is _____

_____

_____

_____

_____

_____

_____

_____

_____

_____

_____

_____.

Fawn is an
animal-talent fairy.

If I could talk to an animal, it would be a

_____.

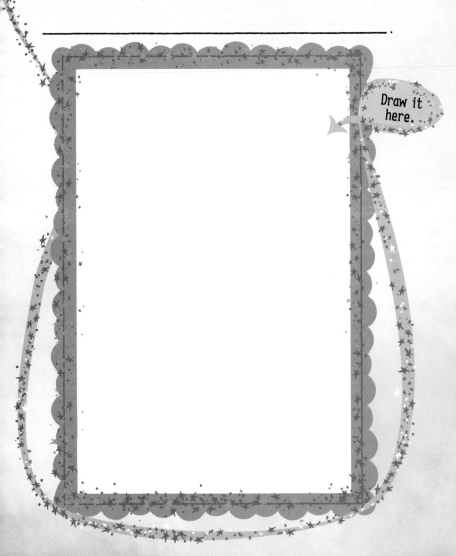

Draw it here.

Rosetta is a garden-talent fairy.

The prettiest garden I've ever seen is_____

_____

_____

_____

_____

_____ .

Draw it
here.

Hem is a sewing-talent fairy.
What kinds of outfits would you like to make?

Draw them
here.

# Quiz: Which Fairy Am I?

1. In my spare time, I like to:
   A) take care of my garden
   B) play with my pets
   C) paint and draw
   D) fix things around the house


2. My friends would say I'm:
   A) prim and proper
   B) natural and fun-loving
   C) creative and artistic
   D) helpful and handy

3. My bedroom is:

    A) neatly decorated with floral prints

    B) filled with stuffed animals

    C) full of inspiration for new projects

    D) cluttered with found objects

4. My biggest flaw is that I'm:

    A) picky

    B) shy

    C) messy

    D) stubborn

If you answered with:

**Mostly As:** You're Rosetta! You love flowers, dresses, and anything pretty, and you're always a proper lady. Sometimes you're so proper that you're a little too fussy.

**Mostly Bs:** You're Beck! You love animals and have a talent for caring for others—but you can be shy around humans.

**Mostly Cs:** You're Bess! You're a true artist who can find inspiration in anything. But sometimes your creative spirit makes you a bit disorganized.

**Mostly Ds:** You're Tinker Bell! You love to fix things and solve problems, especially when it helps your friends. But when someone disagrees with you, you're always sure to let them know you're right.

# Memories

Write about a memory that makes you laugh.

_____

_____

_____

_____

_____

_____

_____

_____

_____

_____

_____

_____

_____

The best vacation I ever went on was _____

_____

_____

_____

_____

_____

_____

_____

_____

_____

_____

_____

_____

_____.

The best birthday I ever had was _____

_____

_____

_____

_____

Draw a picture of the best birthday present you ever got.

My most embarrassing moment ever was _____

_____

_____

_____

_____

_____

_____

_____

_____

_____

_____

_____ .

Everyone makes mistakes.

The biggest mistake I ever made was _____
_____
_____
_____
_____
_____
_____
_____
_____
_____
_____
_____
_____.

The most incredible thing I've ever seen is

_____

_____

_____

_____

_____

_____.

Draw a picture of it here.

my favorite memory with my friends is _____

_____

_____

_____

_____

_____

_____

_____.

# Write about a time when you felt worried.

_____

_____

_____

_____

_____

_____

_____

_____

_____

_____

_____

_____

_____

_____

Write about a time when you felt excited.

_____

_____

_____

_____

_____

_____

_____

_____

_____

_____

_____

_____

The hardest thing I've ever done is _____

_____

_____

_____

_____

_____

_____

_____

_____

_____

_____

_____

_____.

# Have you ever felt stuck? How?

_____

_____

_____

_____

_____

_____

_____

_____

_____

_____

_____

The best thing that's ever happened to me is____

_____

_____

_____

_____

_____

_____

_____ .

The strangest thing that's ever happened to me is

_____

_____

_____

_____

_____

_____

_____

_____.

The sneakiest thing
I've ever done is

_____

_____

_____

_____

_____

_____

_____

_____

_____

_____

_____ .

My favorite memory is _____
_____
_____
_____
_____
_____
_____.

The best vacation I've ever been on was _____
_____
_____
_____
_____
_____
_____
_____
_____
_____
_____
_____
_____ .

The most amazing thing I've ever done is_____

_____

_____

_____

_____

_____

_____.

Here's a picture of the prettiest thing I've ever seen.

Write about a time you felt scared.

_____

_____

_____

_____

_____

_____

_____

_____

_____

I couldn't believe it when _____

_____

_____

_____

_____.

The most special day I've ever had is_____

_____

_____

_____

_____

_____

_____.

# Hopes and Dreams

# when you grow up . . .

What do you want to be?

_____

_____

_____

_____

_____

_____

_____

_____

_____

_____

_____

_____

_____

_____

# when you grow up . . .

Where do you want to live?

_____

_____

_____

_____

_____

_____

_____

_____

# when you grow up . . .

What do you want to see?

_____

_____

_____

_____

_____

_____

_____

_____

_____

_____

_____

_____

_____

# when you grow up . . .

What do you want to do?

_____

_____

_____

_____

_____

_____

_____

_____

_____

_____

# Mind Reader

What do you suppose Fawn is thinking?

Write your ideas
here.

Have you ever dreamed of going to your own
secret world? What would it look like?

Draw it here.

The best day ever would be _____

_____

_____

_____

_____

_____

_____.

Shh! Who's your secret crush?
Write about why you like them.

_____

_____

_____

_____

_____

_____

_____

_____

_____

_____

_____

_____

_____

# Talking with Tink

What do you think Tinker Bell and Kate are saying to each other?

Write your ideas here.

The first time the Never Girls saw Pixie
Hollow, they felt as if they were dreaming.
What is your most marvelous dream?

Write about
it here.

_____

_____

_____

_____

_____

_____

_____

_____

_____

Draw a picture of yourself doing your dream job.

My dream job would be _____

_____

_____

_____ .

One thing I wish I could do is_____

_____

_____

_____

_____

_____

_____ .

A place I would love to explore is _____

_____

_____

_____

_____

_____

_____.

If you were a queen, what would you do?

_____

_____

_____

_____

_____

_____

_____

_____

_____

_____

_____

_____

_____

_____

Gabby thinks fairies can grant wishes.
If you had three wishes, what would they be?

1. _____

_____

_____

_____

_____

_____

2. _____

_____

_____

_____

_____

_____

_____

3.

If you could fly, where would you go? What would you do?

_____

_____

_____

_____

_____

_____

_____

_____

_____

_____

_____

_____

One year from now, I will be _____

_____

_____

_____

_____

_____

_____

_____

_____

_____

_____

_____

_____

_____ .

The date I finished this journal:

My signature:

_____